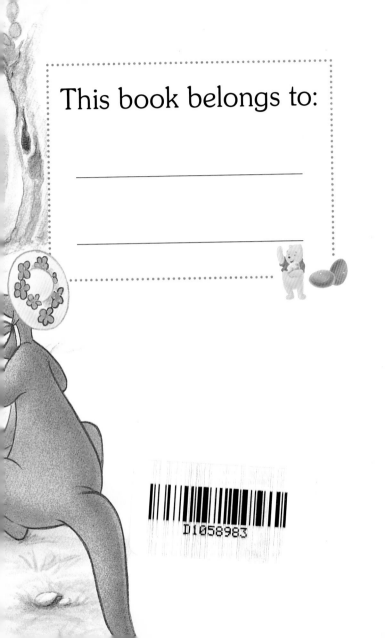

This book belongs to:

_____

_____

D1058983

A catalogue record for this book is available
from the British Library

Published by Ladybird Books Ltd
80 Strand London WC2R 0RL

3 5 7 9 10 8 6 4

A Penguin company

© Disney MMI

Based on the Pooh stories by

A.A Milne (copyright The Pooh Properties Trust)

LADYBIRD and the device of a Ladybird are trademarks
of Ladybird Books Ltd

*All rights reserved. No part of this publication may be reproduced,
stored in a retrieval system, or transmitted in any form or by any means,
electronic, mechanical, photocopying, recording or otherwise,
without the prior consent of the copyright owner.*

# Lost and found

Ladybird

Rabbit

Pooh

egg

Kanga

Tigger

basket

Roo

Eeyore

Piglet

Pooh and his friends were in the woods.

"There are lots of eggs
hidden in the woods," said
Rabbit. "Let's see who
can find the most."

7

Pooh found a yellow egg.

He picked it up and put
it in his basket.

*Plop!*
Out fell the egg.

9

Along came Piglet. He
picked up the yellow egg
and put it in his basket.

10

Then Pooh found a purple egg. He picked it up and put it in his basket.

*Plop!*
Out fell the egg.

Along came Roo. He
picked up the purple egg.

Pooh found a green egg.
He picked it up and put
it in his basket.

*Plop!*
Out fell the egg.

Tigger found the green egg. He picked it up and put it in his basket.

Then Pooh found a red
egg. He picked it up and
put it in his basket.

*Plop!*
Out fell the egg.

Along came Eeyore.

He picked up the red egg.

Then Pooh found a blue egg. He picked it up and put it in his basket.

*Plop!*
Out fell the egg.

Kanga found the blue
egg. She picked it up.

Everyone went back
to Rabbit.
"Let's see who has found
the most eggs," he said.

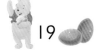
19

Piglet, Roo, Kanga,
Tigger and Eeyore all
had eggs.

Pooh looked in his basket.
There were no eggs.

 21

Pooh was sad.
"Here, Pooh," said Piglet.
"You can have my
yellow egg."

"You can have my purple egg," said Roo.

23

"You can have my green egg," said Tigger.

Kanga gave Pooh the
blue egg, and Eeyore
gave Pooh his red egg.

"Thank you," said Pooh.
"Now let's
have a party!"

RABBITS
HOUSE

"You can eat the eggs," said Pooh, "and I will eat my honey."

And that's just what he did!